PUFFIN BOOKS

Delilah Darling

IS AT THE ZOO

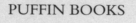

Jeanne Willis wrote her first book when she was
five years old and hasn't stopped writing since.
She has now written over a hundred titles, including
picture books, novels and television scripts.
She has won numerous awards, including the
Children's Book Award, the Sheffield Children's
Book Award and the Silver Nestlé Smarties Prize.
Her teen novel, *Naked Without a Hat*, was
shortlisted for the Whitbread Award in 2003.
She writes with her pet rat keeping her company
and often takes inspiration from dreams and
interesting conversations with strangers.

Delilah Darling

IS AT THE ZOO

Jeanne Willis

Illustrated by Rosie Reeve

PUFFIN

PUFFIN BOOKS

Published by the Penguin Group
Penguin Books Ltd, 80 Strand, London WC2R 0RL, England
Penguin Group (USA) Inc., 375 Hudson Street, New York, New York 10014, USA
Penguin Group (Canada), 90 Eglinton Avenue East, Suite 700, Toronto, Ontario, Canada M4P 2Y3
(a division of Pearson Penguin Canada Inc.)
Penguin Ireland, 25 St Stephen's Green, Dublin 2, Ireland (a division of Penguin Books Ltd)
Penguin Group (Australia), 250 Camberwell Road, Camberwell, Victoria 3124, Australia
(a division of Pearson Australia Group Pty Ltd)
Penguin Books India Pvt Ltd, 11 Community Centre, Panchsheel Park, New Delhi – 110 017, India
Penguin Group (NZ), 67 Apollo Drive, Rosedale, North Shore 0632, New Zealand
(a division of Pearson New Zealand Ltd)
Penguin Books (South Africa) (Pty) Ltd, 24 Sturdee Avenue, Rosebank,

The moral right of the author and illustrator has been asserted

Set in Bembo
Made and printed in England by Clays Ltd, St Ives plc

British Library Cataloguing in Publication Data
A CIP catalogue record for this book is available from the British Library

ISBN: 978–0–141–32282–7

www.greenpenguin.co.uk

Penguin Books is committed to a sustainable future
for our business, our readers and our planet.
The book in your hands is made from paper
certified by the Forest Stewardship Council.

For Joyce Gardiner,
for being marbellous – J.W.

To Rosa and Mariel – R.R.

Chapter One

Hooray, it's me, Delilah Darling. I'm here at last! The reason I am late for school is because I had to run all the way home again. This is because, when I was halfway there, I suddenly remembered I was supposed to bring in one of Daddy's old shirts.

My teacher Mrs Mullet said we all

had to, but I don't know why. I wasn't listening very much because my ears were tired. But it could be important so I specially told my mother to please put the shirt in my school bag, but the poor old sausage forgot.

Her memory is rubbish. The other day, she actually forgot that I come from a land far, far away where I am the queen.

'The King of Smindia gave me two pet rhinoceroos as a gift when I was crowned,' I said. 'Dear old Porky and Pronto, you must remember them, Mother.'

Well, she just looked at me as if *I* was mad and said, 'Must I, Delilah?'

If my own mother can forget enormous things like a rhinoceroo, no wonder she can't remember a little thing

2

like a shirt. In the land where I come from, mothers only forget things you *don't* want them to remember, like when bedtime is or that you have to eat cabbage.

Anyway, because of the shirt not being in my bag, I had to run all the way home to fetch it with Gigi. She is my Old Pear, which means Daddy has to pay her to walk me to school. It's a waste of money really. She can't run uphill because she's French and has to wear high heels. She can run very fast downhill though. And scream loudly at the same time.

She was going gallopy, gallopy, scream with my brother, Smallboy, in his buggy and he thought it was wonderful fun. He shouted, 'Mind out, Lollipop Man, or I will run over your lollipop,' in Far Away Language.

When we got home, there was nobody in except Ambrose my cat and Arnold my dog. My mother, who is an Inferior Designer, had gone to make someone's house look like it wasn't theirs and Daddy was at work playing golf. I didn't know which was his old shirt because they all look old so Gigi just took one from his wardrobe.

'Thees one is *'orrible*,' she said. 'In my country of France, even the Scaredy Crow would not be seen dead in this.'

So I stuffed the Scaredy Crow shirt in

my bag and ran all the way back to school and now I'm here. I'm only a little bit late, but Horrid Charlotte Griggs who is my worst enemy saw me sneaking in.

'Um! I'm telling of you,' she says. 'Mrs Mu-llet, Delilah Darling is late!' And Mrs Mullet asks why I am late, but before I can explain, Horrid Charlotte says, 'I expect it's because she can't tell the time.'

Oh yes I can. It's a-something to twelve, but she says, 'Ha, ha, no it isn't! When the little hand is on the nine, it's a-something to nine. Even an idiot knows that.'

'I don't!' shouts Lucian Lovejoy, who is my boyfriend.

I tell Horrid Charlotte it's not nine o'clock in Far Away Land. The hands go

the *other* way round there
and my best friend Edie
Chadwick says, 'Delilah's
right. And the clocks go
tock tick instead of tick tock.'

'You're making it up,' says Charlotte. 'If
it's really a-something to twelve, it would
be lunchtime here.'

'Good!' shouts Lucian. 'I'm hungry.
Delilah tells the time the way I like it.'

Then Mrs Mullet says, 'Class Two, stop
shouting or you will not be allowed to
make a lovely collage. I hope you've all
brought in old shirts to wear or you'll
get covered in glue.'

We're doing a project all about the
rain forest and we have to make a
normous jungle scene from pictures cut
out of magazines.

'I've brought my daddy's *new* shirt in,' says Horrid Charlotte. 'He never wears old ones because he's rich.'

'It's not your dad's, it's your mum's,' says Edie.

'Oh no it's not!' says Charlotte.

'Oh yes it is. It's a frilly ladies' blouse. Delilah thinks so too, don't you, Delilah?'

Before I can even answer, Mrs Mullet says there's no need for silliness and to please put on our old shirts over our clothes. Then she gives us magazines and tells us to cut out things that live in rain forests.

I'm cutting out a gorilla, Edie is cutting out a snake and Lucian is cutting out a bare lady. When Mrs Mullet asks why he has cut out a bare lady, Lucian says he thought she lived in the rain forest because she's twirling an umbrella, so Mrs Mullet takes his scissors away.

'I am cutting out a little pony,' says Saloni.

'There are no ponies in the rain forest,' says Ben Silverstein who knows everything.

'I'm telling you there are ponies,' says Saloni. 'We went there in Cousin Sindra's motor car and it rained and rained and rained. That is how I know it was the rain forest.'

'I think you went to the New Forest, dear,' says Mrs Mullet. 'In England.'

'Told you!' says Ben Silverstein. 'Rain forests are found in the Amazon, Africa, India and Australasia. Half the world's animals live there, none of which are ponies.'

I'm about to tell him that in the land where I come from, there are millions of ponies in the rain forests, only Mrs Mullet butts in and says she's glad Ben

knows so much because it shows he was listening yesterday when she told us all about it. Then she makes us stop what we're doing because she has something exciting to tell us.

'Ooh!' says Horrid Charlotte. 'Are you getting married?'

'Ooh!' says Lucian. 'Are you marrying Mr Potter?'

Mr Potter is our caretaker, but no one would want to marry him. He's so grumpy, he won't let us jump off the roof or anything.

'No, I'm not marrying Mr Potter,' she says. 'I'm already married to Mr Mullet.'

'But say he leaves you,' says Edie, 'would you marry Mr Potter?'

'I could be your bridesmaid,' says Charlotte. 'Please, can I?'

Mrs Mullet goes ever so red and says we're to stick to the subject of rain forests and Lucian says he *is* stuck to the subject because he's just spilled his glue in his lap. So we all have to wait while he unsticks his pants from his trousers and changes into his P.E. shorts.

'What I'm trying to tell you,' sighs Mrs Mullet, 'is that on Monday, we're all going on a trip to see some real rain-forest animals.'

'Whoop-de-doo! Did you hear that?' says Connor O'Reilly. 'We're all going to the Amazing and the Australasiams and the Wherever Else it was Ben said.'

Everyone is terribly excited about going abroad, but then Mrs Mullet says we're only going on a short coach trip to see them in the zoo and Charlotte

Griggs says, 'Oh poo . . . dles. That's really, really boring.'

But it won't be. When we get to the zoo, Mrs Mullet is going to give us a quiz about rain-forest animals and whoever gets the most answers right wins a prize. Me and Edie are so excited. We love prizes.

'What's the prize?' asks Horrid Charlotte. 'Is it any good?'

'It's a surprise,' says Mrs Mullet.

'It better be a doll's house,' says Charlotte.

Me and Edie are wondering what the prize could be too. We think it might be a rain-forest animal such as a baby elephant, which would be brilliant because I've only got a dog, a cat and hamsters and Edie's only got an old guinea pig.

'I expect that's why we're going on a big coach,' says Edie. 'So we can bring the elephant back. I really hope one of us wins.'

'I'll win,' says Ben Silverstein. 'I know everything, so I know I'll win.'

'I'll win,' says Charlotte Griggs. 'Because I'm Mrs Mullet's favourite.'

'No, I'll win,' says Lucian. 'Because I'm going to cheat.'

Chapter Two

It's Saturday and there's Very Important Shopping to do. This is because Mrs Mullet gave everyone a letter to give to their parents telling them to buy stuff for our zoo trip. My mother was lazing about doing ironing so I read the list out for her.

I thought it was rather kind of me to

save her having to read it for herself and I'm sorry if I interrupted while she was listening to an extremely boring radio play, but there was no need for her to go huff and puff. All I said was this: 'I need a new lunch box, a new raincoat, some sandwiches that aren't cheese and a hundred pounds to spend in the zoo shop.'

Well, my mother folded her arms and said to *show* her where it said about the hundred pounds. Only I couldn't because Mrs Mullet had forgotten to put in the exact sum.

'Everyone else is bringing a hundred pounds,' I told her.

I don't know why she wouldn't believe it, but she said a hundred pounds was far too much money to spend in a zoo shop.

 15

'Not if you want to buy a gorilla.'

I was planning to buy a gorilla in case I didn't win the elephant and Edie was planning to buy an anteater, but when I

explained, my mother just laughed and she said, 'Delilah, darling, they don't sell real animals in the zoo shop. It's against the law.'

I think that's the most ridiculous thing I've ever heard. In the land where I

come from, you can buy any sort of
animal you want from the zoo shop.
As long as it likes you, you can buy a
three-toed gerumph or a snotteroo or a
hippopottymouth or anything and
nobody says, 'Oh no you can't!' or
'Where are you going to put it?' because
of course you put it in your bedroom
with all the others.

So just because of that silly law, all
I'm allowed is two pounds fifty to buy
a pencil with a rubber monkey on the
end. I phoned Edie and asked if her
mother would be giving her a hundred
pounds to buy the anteater.

'No,' she said. 'I'm afraid not.'

'Is it because your mother's a
vegetarian and anteaters eat ants, which
are meaty?'

And Edie said, 'No, Delilah. It's because she's very, very mean.'

I bet Horrid Charlotte's sweet, kind mother gives her two hundred pounds to spend in the zoo shop, which is a waste because Charlotte doesn't even like gorillas, but when I told my mother this, she said, 'You're not having a hundred pounds to buy a gorilla and that's that. I'll buy you a new lunch box, but you don't need a new raincoat. Your old one is fine.'

It is not fine! It is a stinky pack-a-mac, which has a stupid bonnet that I have to tie in a strangle under my chin, and when I wear it Charlotte Griggs calls me Granny Grunt. I told my mother this, but she said, 'Ignore her, Delilah.'

She has no idea how impossible it is

to ignore Horrid Charlotte, so I went stomp, stomp off to Daddy and showed him my best sad face. Now he is taking me shopping – hooray! He's supposed to be putting up shelves, but I don't think he wants to awfully much. My mother likes him to put them up straight, but he likes to put them up wonky.

It is much more fun going to the shops with someone who doesn't know what your mother said you can't have. I carry the basket and Daddy is following behind and I just say things like, 'Mum's been meaning to buy me this doughnut maker for ages' and 'Sadly I have grown out of all my hats' and 'Mrs Mullet says we have to bring in a normous bag of Pic 'n' Mix on Tuesday' and he lets me have anything I want.

I've found the coat section. There are lots of boring black ones and nasty navy ones and I am going flick, flick, groan when suddenly I find a marbellous coat made from pretend tiger fur. It is the only sort of coat to go and see animals of the rain forest in and there are two of them and one of them fits me perfectly if I breathe in.

It has tiger's ears on the hood and it even comes with a matching furry bag with a stripy tail for a handle. It's very expensive, but did Daddy say no, Delilah, it's not even waterproof? No, he did not. He said, 'Yes, yes. If you want. Can we get a move on?'

This is because he's a nice, kind person unlike some people's mothers. I'm making him carry the coat because my basket is full of other things I desperately need like a horse's head on a stick that goes *neighhh* when you press its ear.

All I need now is a new lunch box because my old one won't shut. This is because Lucian needed somewhere to put a dead crow that he found on the school field and when we tried to shut the lid, the crow was too fat and the catch went snap.

Daddy has wandered off to look at the pretty screwdrivers. He has told me to

 21

go and choose a lunch box and meet him at the checkout, only they're all rubbish except for this lovely expensive one with a tiger on the front.

I'm just about to grab it because it matches my new tiger coat when someone pushes me out the way and snatches it and that someone is . . . Horrid Charlotte! I can't even kick her in the shins and wrestle it off her because she's with her dad.

'Mine, I think,' she says, waving it near my head. 'Isn't it the best lunch box ever? It's the last tigery one. You'll have to buy one of those babyish ones. Come along, Daddy.'

So now, all because of her, I've had to buy a lunch box with a stupid fairy on. Oh well, at least my tiger coat will

 22

be a billion times more brilliant than
Horrid Charlotte's.

She'll be so jealous when she sees
me in it.

Chapter Three

It's Sunday. I'm so excited about going to the zoo tomorrow, but I'm sorry to say Daddy is in big trouble. He's been told off for making me choose the tiger coat. My mother said that he should have bought me the nasty navy one because pretend fur lets the rain in.

She wanted to take it back, only I had

already written in the label. I wrote
'Queen Delilah' in fat felt pen and my
mother said, 'Oh darling, whatever did
you do that for?' And I said, 'Because
it's my name.'

For some reason that means Daddy
can't take the coat back and now he has
to put up the shelves as a punishment.
He is being very noisy with his drill and
yelling 'Ouch!' and 'Flimminheck!' and all
sorts of marbellous words and Smallboy is
copying him in Far Away Language,
saying 'Uggik!' and 'Rissles!' and 'Doddit!'

Me and Edie are listening behind the
door. She came round specially to see my
new tiger coat, but that didn't take very
long. Now we've run out of things to do,
so Edie says, 'Think of something,
Delilah.'

'Well, you could help me scratch this stupid fairy off my lunch box.'

Only, it won't come off, not even with my mother's electric toothbrush and bathroom cleaner so she says, 'I know, Let's play "Guess what I've got for my packed lunch tomorrow".'

I guess it's a cheese sandwich, carrot sticks and an apple because that's what she always gets and she goes sulk, sulk, sulk and says, 'It's not fair. My mother won't even let me have a Penguin biscuit.'

I ask her if it's because she thinks they're made from real penguins and she's vegetarian, but Edie says no, it's because her mother is cruel and only pretends to love her.

Edie doesn't even want to know

26

what's going to be in my lunch box
because she gets jealous, so that's the
end of that game. So we sit there and
do more nothing until my mother says,
'If you need something to do, you
could go and give this magazine to
Mrs Woolly Hat.'

In case you don't know, Mrs Woolly
Hat is my oldest friend apart from Nana
and Grandpa Darling. I'm not sure how
old she is. When I asked she said she was
as old as her tongue and a little bit older
than her teeth and she hasn't got many
of those left so I think she's probably
about a hundred and two.

'I think she's older than that,' says Edie.
'She smells older.'

We like the smell of Mrs Woolly Hat.
She smells of cats and cake.

'And whisky,' says Edie. 'Have you ever drunk whisky, Delilah?'

'No. My mother won't let me.'

Edie says hers won't either and when I ask if it's because whisky is made from whisked meat, she says she's not sure.

'But I think whisky's made from whiskers, Delilah. It sounds like it might be.'

We expect that's why Mrs Woolly Hat has so many cats.

'Let's ask her how she makes whisky out of them,' says Edie.

Only, I've thought of something even better to ask. I've been thinking that Mrs Woolly Hat probably knows all about rain-forest animals because in the olden days, when she was an actress, she was in a film called *Jungle Jane*. If we went

28

round and asked her the right sort of
questions, she might give us the right
sort of answers to win the school quiz.

'Good thinking,' says Edie. 'But if I
win, won't it annoy you very much?'

'Yes, but not nearly as much as it will
annoy Horrid Charlotte.'

She deserves
to be annoyed
for snatching
my tiger lunch
box, so we
knock on Mrs
Woolly Hat's
door and say,
'Good
afternoon.
How many
toes does a

sloth have?' and she says, 'Good question,' and then, when we tell her about our rain-forest quiz, she says, 'How very exciting! What's the prize?'

We tell her it's a surprise, but it might be a baby elephant.

'Or a giraffe,' says Edie. 'You never know.'

'I know all about elephants and giraffes,' says Mrs Woolly. 'I could help you win. When I was an actress, I was in a film about the jungle, you know. Would you like to see it?'

So she closes the curtains to make it like the cinema and we watch the film on her video. We ask all sorts of questions and Mrs Woolly Hat gives us all sorts of answers such as, 'That's a reticulated panther,' and 'Lepers cannot change their spots,' and 'Elephants never forget.' Only when we ask what it is that elephants never forget, she can't remember.

'Don't worry,' I tell her. 'My mother has a much worse memory. She forgot I was Queen of Far Away Land. She even forgot about my rhinoceroos.'

'Fancy!' sighs Mrs Woolly Hat. 'Who could forget dear old Potty and Pookle?'

She asks if we have any more questions and Edie says, 'Why hasn't your ginger cat got whiskers?' and Mrs Woolly Hat says, 'Are you talking about Whisky?'

That's the cat's name, only Edie didn't know, so she says, 'How do you make whisky?'

And Mrs Woolly Hat says, 'How do I make Whisky do what?'

So I say, 'Pardon me, Edie, but what has this got to do with rain forests?' and I remind her that the quiz is tomorrow and we still don't know anything about gorillas and there is bound to be a question about them.

'I know a song about gorillas,' says Mrs Woolly Hat. 'Shall I sing it to you?'

So she does and it goes like this:

> *'Gorillas' hands are like a man's*
> *They both have opposable thumbs*
> *That's how they can hold a stick*
> *And scratch their hairy . . .'*

'Tums!' says Edie.

Isn't that the most marbellous song? Lucian is going to love it.

Chapter Four

It's Monday and today is the day that Mrs Mullet is taking us to the zoo to see animals of the rain forest. Only all of us aren't here yet. Horrid Charlotte Griggs isn't here, which is odd, because she always loves to be early. She lines up at least the night before so she can be right at the front of the queue and that's

why she's Teacher's Pet. Only if I was
Mrs Mullet, I'd rather have a pet
tarantula than Charlotte Griggs,
which in case you don't know is a big
fat hairy spider.

The rest of us are in the playground
waiting for the bell and all the girls
have been saying oh, what a lovely tiger
coat, Delilah, and asking to stroke it. I
have stuffed the lunch box
inside my matching
Tiger Bag so no one
can see the silly
fairy on the front.

Mrs Mullet is
taking ages to
come out and tell
us to come in, so
Connor O'Reilly

and Darren Paisley are seeing
how high they can throw
their wellies in the air. In
the land where I come
from, we always play that
game when we're waiting
to be let into the
classroom.

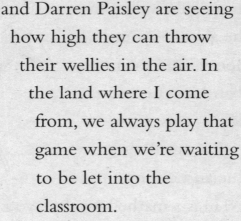

It's called Welly-Uppy.
Everyone wants to play, so
we all stand in a row, take
off our right wellingtons
and hop on our left
feet. Then, after I've
counted one-ga,
toodle, threeba –
which is one, two,
three in Far Away
Language – we

throw our wellies into
the air and shout, 'Go
Booty!' and the one
that doesn't come
down wins.

'I've won!' shouts
Lucian Lovejoy.

He is a marbellous shot, you know.
His welly has landed on the school roof
on top of the weather cock. We're really
happy for him, but Mr Potter isn't. He
comes out of his hut and goes *herumph*
and *pah* and he says, 'Which silly So-
and-So did that? Was it you, Paisley?'

And Darren Paisley, who is normous
for his age, says, 'No, Mr Potter. It was
your mother.' For some reason this
makes Mr Potter even more frowny and
furious and he marches up to Darren

and he says, 'Listen, sonny. If you do that again, I'll . . .'

Only then Mrs Mullet comes out and rings her bell really, really loudly so I never did hear what Mr Potter was going to do to Darren, which is a shame.

Anyway, we all line up and I'm right at the front of the queue and Mrs Mullet says, 'I do hope that coat's waterproof, Delilah. Where's Charlotte?'

And Edie who is standing behind me says, 'I expect Charlotte is late because she's still doing her silly hair.'

And Lucian Lovejoy says, 'I bet she's late because she's been eaten by a bear.'

Then a horrid voice that is all out of puff says, 'I'm weely, weely sorry I'm only just in time, Mrs Mullet, only Mummy left the crusts on my chocolate-

37

spread sandwiches and I had to make her cut them off.'

It's Charlotte Griggs, but far, far worse than that . . . she's wearing the *same* tiger coat as me! She must have sneaked back and bought the last one on purpose.

Only Mrs Mullet doesn't say, 'Oh, I hope it's waterproof,' like she said to me. No, because Charlotte is Teacher's Pet she says, 'Oh, I *do* like your coat. I thought Charlotte was a real tiger for a second, didn't you, children?'

And Edie says, 'I think she looks like Mrs Woolly Hat's old tom cat.'

So Mrs Mullet makes Edie stand at the back of the line and tells Charlotte to come to the front and that horrid girl says, 'De-li-lah. Isn't it funny how two of us can wear the same tiger coat and only one of us looks any good in it?'

I can't even kick her because she's behind me, but Connor O'Reilly can because he's behind her and kicking bottoms is his hobby.

'Any more kicking and you won't be going on the coach!' says Mrs Mullet.

I have never been on a coach before and nor has Edie.

'I wonder what sort of a coach it is,' she shouts. 'Don't you, Delilah?'

Well, I do wonder. We all do. So I tell everybody that in the Far Away Land where I come from, the coaches are made from glass and they are pulled by unicorgis, which are little dogs with wings and curly horns on their noses.

'I can't wait!' says Edie.

Chapter Five

Mrs Mullet has taken the register and we're all here, only we weren't quite sure if Rupert Sinclair-Smythe was all there until just now. Rupert is the smallest boy in the class. He can't even reach his coat peg unless me and Edie lift him up by his belt, so he's very hard to see if he's sitting behind

Huge Darren Paisley. Which he wasn't.

He was sitting *under* Huge Darren Paisley, which is why he did not answer when Mrs Mullet called out his name. She had to give him his asthma puffer because he was a bit wheezy, what with Darren Paisley being such a hefty lump and squishing the air out of him.

Mrs Mullet told Darren never ever to do it again, but he said Rupert Sinclair-Smythe *begged* him to sit on him and when Mrs Mullet asked why, Rupert said, 'I dreamt an elephant sat on me and I wanted to know what it felt like in real life.'

Rupert does say some very strange things. I think it's because his father is a very brilliant professor, but Edie says it's because he's nuts and Mrs Mullet says

that nobody is to sit on anybody,
especially on the coach.

Mrs Mullet tells us all to line up and
walk sensibly because the coach is here.
Only when we get outside everyone's
really disappointed because guess what?
They've sent the wrong coach.

'I'm not getting on that thing!' says
Horrid Charlotte. 'It's not even made
of glass.'

And Saloni says, 'Mrs Mullet, please
where are the unicorgis?'

And Mrs Mullet says, 'What's a
unicorgi?'

How did she ever become a teacher
if she doesn't even know about a simple
thing like that? Even Lucian knows
what a unicorgi is.

'It's a little dog with curly wings and

a horny tail,' he says. 'Ask Delilah.'

'Let's just go and find our seats quietly,' says Mrs Mullet.

Lucian sits next to me and Charlotte Griggs sits in front of us, because she likes to be at the front of everything. Only her silly bunches are dangling over her headrest and annoying us so Lucian undoes one of his sandwiches and sticks bits of sausage in her hair.

After he's done that, he opens his other sandwich, which is egg, only it smells like a stink bomb and Darren Paisley goes *bleuch* and he is sick in his bobble hat.

Mrs Mullet drops the bobble hat in a bucket and puts it next to the driver. Then she tells Lucian to please put the lid back on his packed lunch and swap places with Darren. So Darren comes to the

front and me and Lucian go and sit at
the back, which is great because now we
can pull funny faces at the man in the
car behind.

In the land where I come from, we
always pull faces at the cars behind on
coach trips. It's the rules. Only Lucian
doesn't know the rules and sticks his
tongue out because he thinks he's meant
to. Only when he does that, the blue
light on top of the car behind starts
flashing then it goes *nee-nar nee-nar* and
overtakes our coach.

Lucian's scared the policeman is going to stop and arrest him and then there is a whiffy smell that fills the whole coach and Horrid Charlotte says, 'Mrs Mu-llet? Lucian Lovejoy has opened his lunch box again.'

Only, he hasn't, the lid is still on.

So Edie says, 'You're so wrong, Charlotte Griggs. That smell is coming from a pig farm.'

And Lucian says, 'You're so wrong, Edie. That smell is coming from me. I thought I was going to be arrested, and it made me windy, but I'm all right now the policeman's gone.'

Oh, Lucian. He's so brave. So fearless. No wonder he's my best boyfriend.

Chapter Six

'It's taking so long to get to the zoo, we might as well have gone to the rain forest,' sulks Horrid Charlotte.

'Never mind, we're here now,' says Mrs Mullet. 'Come along, children. Do up your coats and wear your hats . . . no, not you, Darren!'

Too late. Darren Paisley has grabbed

his bobble hat out of the sick bucket and put it back on. So now we have to wait on the coach while Mrs Mullet takes him outside and scrubs his hair with a wet wipe. Just as well he's all spikes and not curls.

Finally we get off and Mrs Mullet counts our heads to make sure none of us have lost one, only someone in Class Two is missing. It's not me, because I'm standing next to Edie and it's not Edie because she's standing next to me and it's not Horrid Charlotte because she's doing silly ballet twirls in her tiger coat, which I think makes her look like a beaver in a bath mat.

'A mad, stripy beaver,' says Edie.

It isn't Connor O'Reilly who is missing either because he's busy spearing

48

Darren's bobble hat with the end of Saloni's umbrella. And it can't be Ben Silverstein because he's trying to see if he can put three cream crackers in his mouth at once.

'Has anybody seen Rupert?' asks Mrs Mullet.

'D'you mean the wee lad who says weird things?' says Connor. 'Only, I put him in the luggage rack. That'll be him banging on the coach window because he can't get down.'

And when Mrs Mullet asks why ever did he put Rupert in the luggage rack, Connor says, 'He begged me. He said if I didn't, he'd get his sister to kiss me.'

I have never met Rupert's sister, but Rupert has and I think Connor would much rather be shouted at by

49

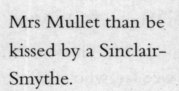

Mrs Mullet than be
kissed by a Sinclair-
Smythe.

She goes off to rescue
Rupert and asks him
what he was thinking
of, begging to be put
in the luggage rack like
that and he says, 'I have
always wondered what
it was like to be a
suitcase.'

'Nut case,' says Edie.

'I think,' says Mrs

Mullet, 'Class Two should stop being silly or I will not be giving out these quiz papers and there will be no prize.'

'Stop being silly everyone!' shouts Charlotte. 'I want to win the doll's house.'

'It won't be a doll's house. That's girly,' says Ben. 'It'll be binoculars.'

'It better not be,' says Charlotte. 'I haven't come all this way to win binoculars.'

Mrs Mullet waits until we all stop wondering what the prize is and when we're quiet, she gives us all a sheet of questions.

'Walk this way, please,' she says.

So we all walk that way and it's a bit annoying because she makes us march straight past the flimmingoes and the

lepers without even saying hello. She says
we can see them later, but I know Mrs
Mullet. Sometimes she says that and
'later' never comes.

'Can we see the alligator later?' asks
Lucian. 'Only, I know a song about that.'

'I was afraid you might,' she says. 'But
we're not going to see the alligators now.
The first question on your quiz is about
chimpanzees, so we're going to see them
first.'

The chimpanzees are really fun only
Charlotte Griggs doesn't like them
because they keep showing us their huge
pink bottoms through the bars.

'Ugh! Mrs Mullet, that one hasn't
even wiped itself!' she squeals.

Mrs Mullet says that's because it's an
ape and it's only natural and tells

everyone to read the first question, only
some of us can't read so she has to say it
out loud: 'Question one. What's the
difference between a monkey and an
ape?'

Connor O'Reilly puts his hand up.

'Is it that apes pick their noses? Only that chimp has got a finger up each nostril and now it's eating it!'

'Euugh!' shrieks Charlotte. 'Darren's copying!'

Mrs Mullet says it's not the right answer and that we're to study the chart on the cage or ask a keeper.

'There's a keeper sitting on that seat behind a tree, Delilah!' whispers Edie. 'You can tell by his hat. Let's get to him before the others do.'

So we run over and ask him what is the difference between an ape and a monkey and he says, 'How the flaming heck should I know? Do I look like a zoo keeper?'

'Yes,' says Edie, pointing to his hat.

'That's a burger hat,' says the man. 'I'm the burger man and I'm on my break. Sling yer hooks, will you?'

'Sling our hooks?' says Edie. 'We haven't got any hooks.'

I think it means he wants us to go away, but Edie refuses and when I tell her there's no point hanging about because he doesn't know anything about apes, she says, 'I know, but he knows about burgers and if we wait, he might make us one.'

Edie's never allowed burgers at home, but she really loves them so when the burger man has finished his cigarette, we follow him to his van and she buys a Double Jungle Whopper. Only, just when she's taken a huge bite, Mrs Mullet comes marching over so I nudge Edie and say, 'Quick! If Mrs Mullet catches you eating a burger she'll tell your mother.'

So she stuffs the whole thing in sideways and when Mrs Mullet sees her cheeks all pouchy, she says, 'Edie Chadwick, what have you got in your mouth?' and Edie says, 'Th'nunning, Mithith Mullik!' and a pickled gherkin shoots out and lands on Mrs Mullet's peep-toe sandal.

'I'm disappointed,' she says. 'Class Two have packed lunches, not burgers. What do you have to say for yourself, Edie?'

Only, she can't speak because she still has a face full of bun. So I have to say it for her.

'Edie's very sorry, Mrs Mullet.'

Edie nods. She isn't a bit sorry though. She'll do anything for a burger, but I have to pretend otherwise Mrs Mullet might not let us go to the Insect House.

Which is where we're off to now.

Chapter Seven

I ask Mrs Mullet if we can see the rhinoceroos on the way to the Insect House. I want to ask them if they know Porky and Pronto, my pet rhinoceroos who live in Far Away Land. But she says we have to do things in order and the next bit of the quiz is about bugs.

'Gross!' says Horrid Charlotte. 'I hate

creepy-crawlies. Will they be loose?'

'The only loose creepy-crawly around here is you,' says Edie.

Mrs Mullet says now, now, girls. No name-calling, please, and she tells Horrid Charlotte not to worry because the insects will be in glass cases.

'Glass breaks though, doesn't it, Mrs Mullet?' says Lucian. 'I know because my sister fell through a glass door and broke it even though I didn't push her. Not hard anyway.'

'It's special glass,' says Mrs Mullet. 'Don't cry, Charlotte.'

We all go into the Insect House. Right at the front there's a normous glass case full of yellow-and-black insects with big eyes and smiley faces and these are called locusts, only there's no question about them in the quiz.

'There's a question about stick insects, Delilah,' says Edie. 'Let's go and find them.'

Well, we found the cage, but it was empty. At least we thought it was, but then Edie says, 'That twig blinked at me. Now it's waving.'

Fancy putting insects that look like twigs in with a load of twigs so they're invisible.

'I hope the prize isn't a stick insect,' says Edie. 'No point having a pet I can't see.'

'You can't miss a baby elephant, Edie. What's the question?'

She looks at the quiz.

'It says, "What do stick insects eat?"'

That's an easy one. They eat sticks.

Otherwise why would they be called stick insects?

'I don't know, Delilah,' she says. 'Shall we just put "They eat sticks" and go and eat our fruit pastilles behind that pillar when no one's looking?'

I think that's a really good idea, and it is, because while we're eating the pastilles, Ben Silverstein sees us. He really likes sweets, only he's not allowed to have them because they make him over-excited so he says, 'If you give me a pastille, I will tell you what stick insects eat – it's leaves.'

We'd put sticks, but he didn't know that, so Edie says, 'We *know* it's leaves. You can only have a pastille if you give us the answer to this question: Name an insect that comes out at night.'

'An antelope,' he says.

'An antelope isn't an insect,' says Edie. 'It's a bird. I'm not dumb. No pastille.'

So Ben goes *tut* and *huff* and then he says, 'All right, then. A firefly – give me a blackcurrant one.'

'How do you spell firefly? Is it with a "ph" or an "f"?'

'Give me another pastille and I'll tell you.'

So we get the answer and the spelling and he gets two pastilles and his eyes go all swivelly and he starts jumping up and down and behaving like Darren Paisley. And when he goes bouncing off, I cross out 'stiks' and write 'leefs' and 'Phire Phly'.

'Ooh!' says Edie. 'That's two we've got right. That's two steps closer to an elephant.'

'It might not be an elephant, Edie.'

It might be a trip to Disneyland in the rain forest or something like that, but Edie isn't sure.

'It might just be a colouring book,' she says. 'Is it worth all this terrible hard work?'

It is worth it though, because even if it is just a colouring book we don't want Horrid Charlotte to have it because of how she took the best lunch box and copied my coat. 'Whatever the prize is, she must not win it, Edie.'

'No, Delilah. We'd never hear the last
of it, would we?'

We are about to go and see the dung
beetle rolling some elephant poop when
Lucian comes running up and says he's
found something even more exciting.

'You know who's in my matchbox,
Delilah?' he says. 'Well, there are millions
of them walking along a piece of wire
and guess what? They are not in a cage.
Quick!'

We run after him, only Mrs Mullet
says, 'No running!' so we jump very fast
and we get round the corner and there
they are — millions and millions of ants
walking along a wire across a pretend
stream and a little garden.

'What have they got in their mouths?'
asks Edie.

'Leafs,' says Lucian. 'They're leaf-cutter ants.'

Lucian is very fond of ants. In fact, he's so fond of them, he always brings some to school in a matchbox and he's just showing them to Edie when Horrid Charlotte arrives and goes: '*Eeeeeeeugh! Arghhhhhhh!*'

Mrs Mullet comes running up, which is a bit naughty of her because she's the one who keeps saying 'No Running!' But anyway she comes running up and she says, 'Whatever's the matter, Charlotte?'

And Horrid Charlotte says, 'There are . . . *waghhhhh* . . . *loose* ants and . . . and . . . Lucian Lovejoy stole some and put them in . . . put them in his . . . mm . . . in his . . . mm . . .'

'In his mouth?' asks Mrs Mullet.

'No, in his *matchbox*!' shrieks Charlotte.

By now a crowd has gathered and Mrs Mullet tells Lucian to give her the matchbox.

'They're my ants,' he says. 'I didn't steal them. They were my grandmother's.'

They were too. He found them in her

sugar bowl. So I tell Mrs Mullet, 'They *are* Lucian's. They're called Gilbert and Wilbur. I'd know them anywhere.'

Lucian opens the matchbox.

'See? That one's Gilbert . . . oh, but I can't see Wilbur. He's run off. Charlotte scared him with all that screaming. Wilbur? Wilbur . . . where are you?'

'You mean one of them's escaped?' yells Charlotte. 'I'm telling my dad of you!'

Mrs Mullet tries to calm her down and I try to find Wilbur because Lucian is so fond of him.

'There's Wilbur!' says Ben Silverstein. 'He's in with the leaf cutters.'

'Oh, grand,' says Connor. 'Wee Lucian's found his ant. Can we eat our lunch now?'

'No,' says Mrs Mullet. 'You are all going to stand still without talking or fidgeting while the zoo keeper removes Wilbur from the wire. Then, if you can behave, we will visit Moonlight World.'

'Is it in outer space?' asks Saloni. 'Only that's a very long way away and Auntie Geeta and Uncle Jit are coming over tonight to show us their holiday photos of the Gambia.'

Mrs Mullet says not to worry, Moonlight World isn't in space; it's at the zoo.

'Can I bring my ants?' asks Lucian.

Mrs Mullet is now doing that thing

where she counts to ten in her head and rolls her eyes.

'Oh. I was hoping you'd say yes,' sighs Lucian. 'Sorry, Wilbur. Sorry, Gilbert.'

Never mind. I'm sure there will be lots of other lovely school trips he can take his ants to. And anyway, he's still got his favourite earwig in the other pocket. It's called Gordon.

Chapter Eight

We are now in Moonlight World. In case you don't know, Moonlight World is a building in the zoo where it's so dark, you can't even see if Darren Paisley is misbehaving. He's playing with his yo-yo. At least I hope that's what he's doing, but it's hard to tell.

'That's not his yo-yo,' says Edie.

'Oh no. Not his potty putty again?'

'I'm afraid so, Delilah.'

I hope he doesn't bounce it too hard and scare the animals.

'I can't even see any animals,' says Horrid Charlotte. 'Why is it so dark in here?'

'Because it's night-time,' says Saloni.

'It's *not* night-time,' says Horrid Charlotte. 'It's only a-something past eleven.'

Mrs Mullet looks at her watch and says, 'Charlotte is right. It's only half past eleven.'

'You see? It is nearly midnight,' yawns Saloni. 'Mummy and Daddy will be wondering where I am. They will think I've been eaten by a tiger.'

'It is not nearly midnight,' Mrs Mullet explains. 'It is nearly midday.'

'Why's it so dark then?' asks Connor O'Reilly. Then Rupert Sinclair–Smythe goes *squeak, squeak, squeak* in his tiny voice and Mrs Mullet says, 'Pardon, Rupert? Speak up, dear.'

So he stands up as tall as he can, which is not much bigger than Smallboy, and he shouts, 'THE REASON IT'S DARK IS BECAUSE MARTIANS HAVE STOLEN THE MOON AND IT'S THE END OF THE WORLD!'

Saloni starts crying and Charlotte starts crying and children who don't even go to our school start crying and Rupert Sinclair–Smythe is still shouting, 'IT'S THE END OF THE WORLD!'

'No it isn't. Shush! He's just making it up,' says Mrs Mullet. 'Rupert has a very vivid imagination.'

But by now everyone in Moonlight World is crying and trying to run out of the exit at the same time and it's all terribly loud and squished and exciting when suddenly – *SNAP!* The lights

come on and the Chief Zoo Man
stands there looking ever so cross. He
says it is not the end of the world, but it
will be the end of our trip if we don't
stop running about and screaming.
Then something small and round goes
bink! off his head and Mrs Mullet hisses,
'Darren Paisley, give me that potty putty!'

'Ooh!' says Edie, 'Look at all the animals!'

Everyone looks all around and we all go 'Wow!' because there are lots of very amazing animals, which we couldn't see before, going blink, blink, blink because the lights are too bright.

'The animals in here only come out at night,' says the Chief Zoo Man. 'We keep them in darkness during the day so they think it's time to get up and you can see them.'

'*I* couldn't see them,' moans Charlotte. 'I want my money back.'

'Once your eyes get used to the dark, you'll be able to,' says the Chief Zoo Man. 'Most of the creatures are very shy, so you have to be patient.'

'I'm very patient,' says Charlotte.

'So am I,' says Lucian. 'Can you hurry up and turn the lights off please?'

When the lights go back off, me and Edie try and find some more answers to our quiz. We're off to find a sloth to count its toes. Mrs Woolly Hat said they have three toes, but I'm not so sure.

'If a sloth has three toes, how many would it have on each foot, Edie?'

'I don't know. It could have one on the left foot and two on the right.'

But it could have three on one foot and none on the other.

'But then it would fall over,' says Edie.

But it wouldn't fall over because sloths don't really stand. They just hang upside down.

'I think that's bats, Delilah.'

'I think you're bats, Edie.'

Anyhow, we find the sloth and count
its toes.

'There are three on each foot,' says
Edie. 'And it's got five feet.'

Only, it hasn't got five feet, it's got two
feet and two hands. The thing Edie
thought was another foot was its tail.

But it's called a three-toed sloth
on the cage, so we can't decide
what answer to put.
Should it be three
toes? Or two times
three toes, because
it's got two feet?

'Delilah, what
is two times three?'

'It's five. At least
it is where I come
from.'

'But what if it isn't five and what if it's three? Charlotte will win the elephant.'

So I write down a scribbly number that looks like it could be a five or a three. It's what we call number thrive in my Far Away Land.

'That's a much cleverer answer than anything Horrid Charlotte could think of,' says Edie.

Just then Lucian comes running up.

'No running!' says Mrs Mullet.

So Lucian hops instead and says, 'Delilah? I'm stuck on question ten. What do fruit bats eat?'

I'm sure it's fruit. Why else would it be called a fruit bat? But Edie isn't certain.

'Perhaps it called a fruit bat because it looks like a piece of fruit, such as a banana. Animals aren't always named after what they eat, are they, Delilah?'

Not in this country. But they are in the land where I come from. There's a cauliflower chicken who eats cauliflowers and a jellyfish who eats jelly and a butterfly who eats butter.

'Does the butterfly also eat margarine?' asks Lucian.

'My mother makes me eat margarine,' says Edie.

I ask if it's because her mother is too mean to buy butter and she says no, it's because she's a vegetarian. Well, I knew that. But what I didn't know is what fruit bats eat and, just as we're about to find out, Mrs Mullet says it's time to go and have our packed lunch.

'I'll tell you what a fruit bat eats if you give me the rest of your fruit pastilles,' says Ben Silverstein.

So I do and he puts them all in his mouth at once. I bet he'll be sick on the coach on the way back.

'Yes,' says Edie. 'And he hasn't even got a bobble hat.'

Chapter Nine

Mrs Mullet says we can eat our packed lunches outside by the fountain. I am glad about that, because then we can watch the animals while we're eating. Mrs Mullet says we will be able to see the gibbons from there. In case you don't know, a gibbon is a little ape with very long arms who likes to sing.

'That's not a gibbon, Delilah,' says Edie. 'That's Lucian.'

On the way to the fountain, we visit the rhinoceroos. I ask one of them, who is called Jambo, if he knew of my pets Porky and Pronto and he swivels his ears and stamps his hoof and says, 'Phthhhher fuff gnunk.'

'Does he remember them?' asks Edie.

'Oh yes. That's what he just said. Rhinoceroos never forget, you know.'

'I thought Mrs Woolly Hat said that was elephants.'

I think it must be both, because Jambo remembered my rhinoceroos perfectly. I'm so glad because my mother thought I was imagining them and now I know I wasn't because Jambo told me so. I can't wait to see her face when I tell her.

When we get to the fountain, there's not much room to sit because children from other schools got there first, so Mrs Mullet says we have to spread out. I ask if me and Edie can go and sit by the flimmingoes and she says yes, but we're not to wander off.

'Can I come?' asks Saloni. 'Only Connor O'Reilly keeps kicking me in the botty.'

So Saloni comes with us and we sit by the flimmingoes, which would have been marbellous only there is a lady and a man kissing on the bench where we want to sit.

'Shall we watch them instead?' asks Edie.

Well, I don't want to because once I saw my Old Pear Gigi kissing her

boyfriend who is called Etienne and
it is not something I like to watch
when I am eating.

'Let's sit over there, on that round
wall,' says Edie. 'That looks like a nice
spot.'

She's right. It's a very nice spot
because when we sit down, we can't see
Mrs Mullet at all.

'Does that mean we've wandered off?'
asks Edie. I don't think it does, because
we can still hear her. She is shouting at
Darren Paisley.

'He has fallen in the fountain,' says
Saloni. 'I heard a big splosh. Connor
O'Reilly must have kicked him in.'

The round wall that we're sitting on
is ever so interesting. It's not just a
wall, there's a deep pit inside it with

grass and rocks and a pool. In the middle there is a normous tortoise the size of a table.

'It must eat ever such a lot of lettuce,' says Saloni.

'Poor thing,' says Edie. 'I hate lettuce.'

There are also some animals, which look like little dragons, sunbathing on the rocks.

'I wonder what's in that cave at the back,' Edie says. 'Is it big dragons, Delilah?'

'No, Edie. Dragons are make-believe animals.'

Saloni looks worried though.

'I am telling you, they are not make-believe, I saw one in a film. It was so scary I had to hide my eyes in Auntie Sindra's cardigan. I am not sitting here if there's a dragon. What does that sign say, Delilah?'

I read it very carefully and it says, 'Reptile Pit'.

'A dragon isn't a reptile, is it, Delilah?' asks Edie

'No, it's a make-believe so it's not allowed to live in this pit. So it can't eat us.'

Saloni opens her lunch box. She's got meat samosas.

'I wish I had meat samosas,' sighs Edie. 'My mother never gives me meat samosas.'

'Is it because she is Scottish?' asks Saloni.

So I say, 'No. It's because she's vegetarian.'

And Edie says, 'No, it's because she

hates me. Why else would she put celery spread in my sandwiches? I wonder if dragons like celery?'

Before I can even answer, she throws her sandwich right into the pit.

'Oh, dear me. I don't think you should have done that, Edie Chadwick,' says Saloni.

She should not have, either, because there's another sign over there, which says 'Do Not Feed the Animals', only Edie didn't see it and when I read it out loud to her, she says, 'But why can't we feed them?'

I don't know, but even in the land where I come from, if you feed the zoo animals you always get into trouble, especially if you give them celery.

'If the keeper sees you,' says Saloni, 'he will tell Mrs Mullet and she will not let you do the quiz and Horrid Charlotte will win the prize, which is possibly a pony or a racing car.'

Edie thinks very hard then she says, 'Give me your umbrella, Saloni.'

'Why? It isn't even raining.'

But the umbrella does have a very long hooky handle and Edie says, 'I'm going to hook the sandwich out of the pit. Tell me if the keeper's coming.'

I keep a lookout for the keeper while Edie tries to hook out the sandwich with the umbrella only she

can't quite reach, so she leans over and suddenly Saloni screams, 'Aieee! There's a crocodile in the pool!'

And Edie
falls right into
the reptile pit
and Saloni runs
off shouting, 'Mrs
Mullet! Mrs Mullet!
Edie Chadwick is
being eaten by
a crocodile!'

'Mega!' shouts Darren
Paisley. 'Can we watch?'

Mrs Mullet, Class Two, all the classes
who aren't even in our school and the
Chief Zoo Man all come running over
to see if there's anything left of Edie, but
by the time they get there, I've pulled
her out.

'It's all right, Mrs Mullet,' says Edie.
'I'm alive.'

'That is soooo disappointing,' says Horrid Charlotte.

'That is not a crocodile,' says the Chief Zoo Man. 'It's an iguana. It's a harmless vegetarian.'

I tell him Edie's mother is a vegetarian, but Edie says, 'Only, *she* isn't harmless, Delilah.'

Edie is furious with her mother. If she'd made her some nice sandwiches with chocolate spread instead of celery, Edie would never have thrown them to the dragons and nearly got eaten by a crocodile that wasn't.

'Who threw that sandwich in the pit?' asks the keeper. 'Was it you, young lady?'

Saloni shakes her head. 'No, no. I would have thrown my samosas.

93

I don't like the onions in them.'

'I bet it was Delilah Darling,' says
Horrid Charlotte. 'I bet they always
throw sandwiches at the crocodiles in
her stupid Far Away Land.'

Edie looks up at the sky and for
some reason the keeper looks at *me* and
he says, 'Did you throw that sandwich?'
and I say, 'What sandwich?'

And when he turns round,
there isn't a sandwich.
This is because the
normous tortoise
ate it all when he
wasn't looking.

It's ever so smiley because, even though celery's horrible, I expect it makes a marbellous change from lettuce, lettuce and more lettuce.

'There's a reason why that sign says "Do Not Feed The Animals",' says the Chief Zoo Man. 'If they're given the wrong food, it can make them ill. It can even make them behave oddly, like children who have had too many sweets.'

'Edie Peedie Weedie!' says Ben Silverstein. 'Got any more pastilles?'

Chapter Ten

After lunch, Mrs Mullet takes us to
The Activity Centre. I thought it
was a place where we had to do acting,
but it's not. It is a place where we have
to be quiet and sit still and listen to a
man with a beard called Mr Bunsen
who keeps telling us off.

He told me and Edie off for lifting

Rupert Sinclair-Smythe up by his belt
so he could hang his coat up. Mr Bunsen
said it was dangerous and when I said,
'Is it because there's a fierce rain-forest
animal lurking in this cloakroom?' he
said, 'No, it's dangerous because you
might drop him.'

Well, of *course* we might drop him. We
often do. Rupert doesn't mind a bit
because he hasn't got very far to fall, but
when we tried to explain, Mr Bunsen
told us to put him down and sit on a
stool and face the front.

'I'm facing the front, Mr Bunsen!' says
Charlotte Griggs.

'Excellent!' he says. 'You can give out
the paper and crayons.'

I wanted to give out the paper and
crayons, but no. Horrid Charlotte gets

 to give them out,
even though she
faced the front
just to be
annoying. In the
land where I
come from, the
queen, which
is me, always gets
to give out the
paper and crayons and Charlotte Griggs
isn't even a princess.

'I'll tell you what Charlotte Griggs is,'
says Edie, 'she's a poisonous tree frog.'

Mr Bunsen must have heard her
because then he says, 'OK, kids. What
do we know about poisonous tree frogs?'
and Ben Silverstein puts his hand up
and says, 'They're frogs that are

poisonous and they live in trees.'

Mr Bunsen scratches his beard and says, 'R . . . right. What else do we know?'

Saloni puts her hand up and says, 'I have something nasty on the end of my umbrella.'

Then Rupert Sinclair-Smythe stands on his stool and goes mumble, mumble, mumble because he has a little voice to match his little self and when Mr Bunsen asks him to speak up, Rupert shouts, 'WHAT IF POISONOUS TREE FROGS ARE REALLY ALIENS WHO ARE PLANNING TO TAKE OVER OUR UNIVERSE?'

Mr Bunsen doesn't really know what to say to that, so Mrs Mullet says, 'Class Two, Mr Bunsen has very kindly given up his time to tell us about rain-forest animals, so if anybody has a *sensible* question to ask him, put your hand up.'

So Lucian puts both hands up and he says, 'Yoo hoo? Mr Bunsen, is your beard real or is it made from cotton wool?'

Well, his beard did look like cotton wool, but Mrs Mullet said it was the silliest question she'd ever heard and made Lucian sit next to her, which was annoying because then we couldn't play with his earwig or anything.

After that, we all have to watch Mr Bunsen's slide show about rain forests. It's really boring until he clicks on a wrong slide and says, 'Here is a hippo wallowing in the Congo River.'

Only, it isn't, it's his wife in a pink

swimming costume
and goggles, but
for some reason,
we aren't allowed

to giggle. This is very odd, because in
the land where I come from, if
something is funny, we laugh and laugh
and laugh and nobody ever says, 'Class
Two! If I hear any more giggling, you
will *not* be making animal masks.'

'I'm not giggling, Mrs Mullet!' says
Charlotte Griggs.

So of course *she's* allowed to hand out
the glue and the feathers and elastic.
Edie doesn't like that one bit because
she knows I'm the queen and she thinks
I should have been asked to hand things
out, so she says, 'Delilah, if some people
keep being allowed to hand out feathers

and glue, other people should be allowed
to glue feathers to that person's big
behind, don't you think?'

'Yes, Edie, I *do* think!'

So when no one was looking, that's
exactly what Other People did, only
nobody knew it was them because they
were wearing animal masks at the time.

I made a marbellous mask of a tiger

and Edie made quite a good mask of
a buffoon and Lucian made a very
clever mask indeed. It started off as a
panda, but Mr Bunsen said pandas didn't
live in the rain forest, which is odd,
because where I come from, you can't
move for pandas in the rain forest, but
Mr Bunsen seemed to think I was
imagining things.

Lucian was so cross about no pandas, he took his panda mask, snipped off the ears and went scribble, scribble, scribble over the white furry bits with black crayon and when Mr Bunsen asked what it's meant to be, Lucian said, 'A poisonous tree frog tadpole.'

'A tadpole?' said Mr Bunsen. 'Only it's a little hard to tell . . .'

Lucian rolled his eyes and went *tut* and said, 'That's because you've got it upside down.'

When everyone has done their masks, we put them on and Mrs Mullet takes a photo of us and says, 'Smile, everyone!' and Ben Silverstein says, 'Smile? How can she see if we're smiling if we're wearing masks? Pass it on!'

So we pass it on and we all pull

secret silly faces behind our animal masks because no one can see us. Only everyone saw Charlotte Grigg's silly face because the elastic on her mask went ping for some reason, which Lucian says was nothing to do with him.

Mrs Mullet wasn't very pleased with Horrid Charlotte's face, so now she's not allowed to wear her mask, which is a shame because she looks much better with it on.

'Where are we going next?' asks Edie. 'Only, I'd like to get on with this quiz.'

'The Parrot House,' says Mrs Mullet. 'To help with your questions, there are speaking buttons by the cages. If you press them, they will tell you all about that animal.'

'Really?' says Connor O'Reilly.

'Speaking buttons! Wow, I never knew that.'

'Oh, you don't know *anything*,' groans Horrid Charlotte.

'I know something you don't know,' he says. 'You've a feather stuck to your bum.'

She didn't know, either, and she was furious, but when she asked Edie who put the feather there and was it Delilah Darling, Edie just grinned behind her buffoon mask and said, 'I'm not telling because . . . you're horrid.'

Which is the only thing to say to a girl like Charlotte.

Chapter Eleven

I am having such a fun day at the zoo. I haven't learnt much about rain-forest animals, but I know what a crocodile isn't and I know that if you kick Darren Paisley in the bottom he will fall in the fountain and I know that I mustn't feed the animals or they will behave like Ben Silverstein.

We are now in the Parrot House, but it's a bit boring because the parrots won't talk to me. I've said hello to the grey one three times, but it won't answer. I think it's because it's shy, but Horrid Charlotte says no wonder it doesn't want to talk to me.

'I wouldn't talk to a girl who had a stupid fairy on her lunch box either,' she says.

It's a mean and horrid thing to say. I have still not forgiven her for wearing the same tiger coat as me and that is why I have taken mine off. I've given it to Lucian to wear. It looks much more marbellous on him than it does on her, especially with the hood up. Mrs Mullet doesn't know it's Lucian in the tiger coat and when he does something bad

– like he's doing now – she thinks it's Horrid Charlotte and she says, 'Charlotte, don't do that. It's not very ladylike.'

It's a bit hilarious because Charlotte Griggs isn't even doing anything wrong except for breathing and she doesn't know why she's being told off.

'It's not me, Mrs Mullet, it's Delilah!' she says.

But it isn't me, because I'm hiding behind the parrot cage and Charlotte still doesn't know it's really Lucian in my tiger coat.

'Delilah,' says Edie. 'We have to stop laughing now because we need to fill in our quiz. Otherwise you-know-who-is-horrid will win and what if the prize is a year's supply of sherbet fountains?'

'Well, she's not having those, Edie. What answer do we need to find?'

'What colour is a toucan's beak.'

'It's *bill*,' says Ben Silverstein.

So off we go to see what colour Bill the Toucan's beak is. In case you don't know, a toucan is a bird that has a beak like a banana.

'Bill!' says Ben. 'It's called a bill, not a beak.'

I know that a beak is called a bill really. I was just testing Ben Silverstein to see if he was being more like himself now that he had stopped eating Edie's pastilles.

'Aha!' says Edie when we get to the toucan cage. 'Bill's bill is yellow.'

'He is not called *Bill*!' shouts Ben.

'I shall call him whatever I like,' says

Edie. 'His name is Billy Bollow, isn't it, Delilah?

And I say yes, because she's my best friend.

'It's short for William,' I tell Ben.

'It's a stupid name,' says Charlotte Griggs who has been listening and Billy Bollow goes *squawk*, *squawk* and says a very rude word.

'Isn't that the word your dad said when he was putting up shelves, Delilah?' says Edie.

I can't remember. Daddy said all sorts of new words that day. Then Billy Bollow says it again and again and soon all the children, including all the children who don't even go to our school, are standing round the cage and saying it back.

'Mrs Mullet! Mrs Mu–llet!' shouts
Horrid Charlotte. 'Delilah Darling has
been teaching the toucan a very rude
word.'

Along comes Mrs Mullet and she says,
'Who's being rude?'

And Charlotte points at me and says,
'It's her!'

So Edie points at the toucan and says, 'It's him!'

Then Ben Silverstein says, 'It's Darren.'

It is too! Darren Paisley is hiding behind a pillar pretending to be the voice of Billy Bollow saying rude words and when Mrs Mullet finds out she isn't pleased at all and she says, 'If you don't behave, you will *not* be allowed to buy anything in the zoo shop later.'

That shut him up straight away. Darren wants to buy a hairy bird-eating spider and he'll be sad if he's not allowed because then he won't be able to put it in his nan's bed.

'Come along,' says Mrs Mullet. 'Everybody line up. Let's go to the Snake House.'

'Did she say snack house or snake house?' asks Lucian. 'Only, I'm hungry.'

He can't hear very well because he's wearing my tiger coat with the hood up still and everything is a bit muffled.

'She said "snack". Can't you hear anything?'

'I can hear *some* things,' he says. 'I heard that toucan say b . . .'

He shouts out the rude word and Mrs Mullet sees the tiger coat and says,

'Charlotte, if I hear that word once more, I shall tell your parents!'

I do love my teacher.

Chapter Twelve

On the way to the Snake House, we're going to see the Big Cats. My cat Ambrose is big. This is because he eats one dinner at my house and another dinner at Mrs Woolly Hat's.

Even so, he is not nearly as big as the big cats we are going to visit, which are called lions, tigers, lepers and jugulars.

'It's jaguars,' says Ben Silverstein.

It's jugulars where I come from, but I haven't got time to argue with him because I can't find Lucian. He was here a minute ago, but then he just . . . went.

'He's probably looking for creatures to put in his other matchbox,' says Edie.

I expect she's right. Lucian will be missing Gilbert and Wilbur now that Mrs Mullet has taken them and even though he still has Gordon, it's not the same. He loved those ants.

'They were rather special, Delilah,' sighs Edie. 'Such dear little faces.'

'Edie, do you know how many toes a sloth has please?' asks Saloni. 'Only, my pencil broke in Moonlight World and I forgot to write it down.'

'Nine,' says Edie. 'Do you know which Big Cat runs the fastest?'

'Yes. It is the cheetah.'

I write it down and say thank you very much to Saloni because that's saved us having to do lots of reading.

'Thank you for the number of sloth toes also,' she says.

Edie Chadwick is a bit bad sometimes. She knows sloths don't have nine toes and when I ask her why she gave Saloni the wrong answer, she says, 'Isn't it nine? I thought that's what it was.'

But really it's because she doesn't want anyone to win the quiz except us, but we like Saloni so I stare at Edie very hard until she knows I know she's been not very kind.

'It wasn't a fib, it was a forget,' says

Edie. 'If I give Saloni the right answer to what a lady lion is called, will you stop staring at me?'

'I might.'

So we run along and find Saloni watching the lepers and whisper that she has put down the wrong answer to the question about lady lions.

'A lady lion is called a lioness,' says Edie. 'Not Mrs Lion.'

'Isn't it?' says Saloni. 'Could I borrow your rubber, please?'

Well, I can't lend her my rubber because it's in my coat pocket and Lucian is wearing my coat and I don't know where he is to get it back.

'I haven't seen him for ages,' says Saloni. 'Maybe he's gone to find a caterpickle to put in his matchbox.'

'That's what I think too,' says Edie.

So we didn't think any more about Lucian and we were just pressing the Speaking Button to find out more things about lions, such as what they eat and how much they weigh, when Mrs Mullet says to come and see the tigers.

'Tigers eat people! They won't be loose, will they?' whines Horrid Charlotte.

'Good heavens, no,' says Mrs Mullet.

'That's what you said about the ants,' scowls Charlotte. 'And look what happened.'

Mrs Mullet tells her that the tiger enclosure has great big bars with pointy bits at the top so they can't get out.

'Has one *ever* got out though?' asks Charlotte.

Mrs Mullet doesn't think so, but Ben Silverstein does.

'If they never get out, what are those red emergency buttons for?' he says.

And Rupert Sinclair-Smythe goes *squeak, squeak, squeak* and Mrs Mullet asks him to please speak up and he says, 'Once a mad man climbed into the tiger cage . . .' Then he didn't say anything.

'Really?' says Mrs Mullet. 'What happened?'

'Yeah, what happened?' asks Darren Paisley. 'Only, I was thinking of climbing in. I know where a rope is — it's in with the gibbons.'

'Rupert,' says Ben. 'What happened? Was the mad man eaten by the tiger?'

'I am not allowed to tell you,' says Rupert. 'If I do, my eyes will explode.'

It's so annoying because we all really want to know. Edie offered him the answer to where do babies come from and Saloni offered him a samosa and I offered him the key to my golden palace in Far Away Land, but he still wouldn't tell.

'Leave Rupert alone, please, everybody,' says Mrs Mullet. 'The tigers can't escape.'

Only, just as she said that, Horrid

Charlotte went a really horrid colour
and started pointing at a bush near the
tiger cage.

'Aghhhhh! Look! One's got out!'

We all looked and we *could* see a
tiger tail and Mrs Mullet says, 'Oh, don't
be so silly. It's just Delilah in her tiger
coat.'

But then Charlotte points at me and
says, 'No, Mrs Mullet, there's Delilah,
right there! She hasn't got a coat on!'
and she screams, 'Help, help, a tiger has
got out!'

Now all the children in the class and
all the children who aren't in our class
are shouting help, help and then Darren
Paisley shouts, 'Don't worry, I'll break
the glass on the alarm. I'm good at
breaking things.'

He goes *smash* and
the alarm goes *BRRRR-
RRRRRRRRRRRRR*
and the Chief Zoo Man
arrives in his van and he
goes, 'Not you lot again!'

'I expect he'll shoot that tiger,' says
Ben Silverstein.

The keeper gets out of the van by the
bush where the tiger tail is and Edie
nudges me and whispers, 'Delilah, are
you thinking about someone who went
missing in your tiger coat and
wondering if there's been a normous
mistake?'

So I run up
to the zoo
keeper and I
grab him
round the
knees and I
shout, 'Don't
shoot! It's
not a real
tiger . . .'

It's my best boyfriend Lucian Lovejoy.
He must have got hot in my coat and
fallen asleep watching the Big Cats. The
keeper prods him with a stick to make
sure and Lucian wakes up and rubs his
eyes. He looks ever so confused.

'Why is everybody screaming?' he
yawns. 'It's only me.'

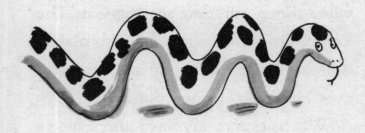

Chapter Thirteen

There's no time to visit the Snake House now. Lucian is furious because he wanted to squeeze the python, which is a normous snake with eyes at one end and a tail at the other end. It's too late to see it because the Chief Zoo Man took so long telling us off.

It's all Horrid Charlotte's fault. If she wore her glasses like she's meant to, she would never have mistaken poor Lucian for an escaped tiger and scared everybody like that.

Never mind. We are going to what is called The Children's Zoo. In case you don't know, The Children's Zoo is where they keep all the naughty kids in cages.

DO NOT FEED
DANGER

At least it is in the land where I come from, but Ben Silverstein says it's not a bit like that here.

'The Children's Zoo,' he says, 'is where they put the boring animals.'

He is so wrong. The Children's Zoo is brilliant. There is a very interesting horse with four legs and green teeth and some marbellous sheep that make olives. At least, Darren Paisley said they were olives, but when Connor picked one up off the ground and tested it, it wasn't an olive at all.

'Mrs Mullet? Connor O'Reilly is eating sheep poo,' shouts Horrid Charlotte.

Well, I don't think he ate it and nor does Edie and nor does Connor. He says he just sniffed it and put it in his pocket, but Mrs Mullet still made him wash his hands.

As well as the horse and the sheep there is a normous mummy pig lying down in the straw. She has pink buttons all down her front with lots of piglets stuck to them.

'Euggh!' says Horrid Charlotte. 'Those smelly little pigs are eating the big one.'

'No, they are not,' says Ben Silverstein. 'They're drinking pig milk.'

'Pig milk, I wonder what it tastes like?' says Connor O'Reilly. 'Do you think it tastes of bacon, Mrs Mullet? I think I'll have a sniff.'

Before Mrs Mullet can answer, he bends over to sniff and a marbellous creature called a Billy Goat's Gruff comes gallopy gallopy and butts Connor

O'Reilly right up his bottom. He goes
waaaagh and falls head over heels into the
pig pen and we all shout '*Yaaaay!*'
because he is always kicking us up the
bottom and now he knows how it feels.

'That'll teach you,' says Edie Chadwick. 'You kicked me when I was the back end of the horse in our play called *The Gingerbread Man*.'

'And you kicked me in the fruit bats,' says Saloni.

'And you kicked me in the fountain,' says Darren.

While Mrs Mullet takes Connor O'Reilly off to the medical room to put an ice pack on his Billy Goat's butt, we go inside to see what other animals live there.

'I bet it's a gorilla, don't you, Delilah?' says Edie. But it isn't. It's a slow worm and a newt and an oven where they cook tiny yellow chicks.

'It's not an oven,' says Ben Silverstein. 'It's an incubator for hatching eggs.'

'Delilah knows that,' says Edie.

Of course I know that. I'm just testing him. I think the pastilles have worn off now because Ben Silverstein is back to his annoying, know-all self again. I'm so glad Lucian is my boyfriend and not Ben because even if Lucian knew something clever, no one would ever know. Right now, he's petting The Children's Zoo mouse.

'I do love this mouse,' he says. 'I would love to keep it, Delilah.'

'Ugh,' says Horrid Charlotte. 'Mice are smelly. Wash your hands, Lucian Lovegerm.'

We are just about to put sawdust in her hair when suddenly Darren Paisley says, 'Oh . . . what? That's mega!'

And in comes the Children's Zoo

Keeper Man with a normous python around his neck. Mrs Mullet is ever so kind because even though *some* of us haven't behaved and we know who we are, she's asked the keeper to show us his snake because there are snake questions in our quiz.

'Ah,' whispers Edie. 'Here's one, Delilah. What kind of snake snuffocates its prey?'

'A Not Very Friendly Snake, Edie.'

Then the keeper says, 'The python isn't poisonous. It's a constrictor, which means it suffocates its prey by squeezing it in its coils.'

'Write down "constrictor",' hisses Edie. 'How many questions are left?'

There's only one and it's about a cockatoo, only we forgot to find the answer in the Parrot House because we were having such fun with Billy Bollow, the rude toucan.

Edie asks Mrs Mullet if we can go back to the Parrot House, but she says no, after we've seen the python we're going to the gift shop and then we are going home on the coach.

'Delilah,' says Horrid Charlotte. 'If you haven't got all the answers it's your silly fault for misbehaving.'

Which means she must have all the parrot answers and we haven't.

'Oh no! She'll win the luxury yacht and the matching tree house!' gasps Edie.

We think that's what the prize is now. Charlotte mustn't win, so Lucian says he'll go to the toilet and on the way he will find out the answer to the cockatoo question by accidentally looking at Ben Silverstein's quiz sheet.

Lucian puts his hand up so nicely, Mrs Mullet lets him go and while he

isn't here, a very exciting thing happens.
We're allowed to stand in a line and hold
the python on our shoulders. It does feel
very lovely and dry like a hot water
bottle and not a bit slimy.

'Why do I have to get to hold its
stinky tail end?' moans Horrid Charlotte.

I tell the snake to snuffocate her, only
sadly it doesn't hear me because it's got
no ears.

Chapter Fourteen

Lucian has just come back from the
toilet. He looks very pleased with
himself and when I ask him did he find
the answer to the cockatoo question, he
says, 'Yes, and I found an even better
thing.'

'Ooh! What sort of better thing?'

'It's in my pocket,' he says. 'Feel it.'

Well, I'm just about to feel it when Mrs Mullet says that it's time to go.

'But we haven't seen the gorillas,' I tell her.

She says we will see them quickly on the way to the gift shop. Only I don't want to see them quickly. I want to stay and talk to them for ages because they're my favourites.

'You could buy a stuffed one,' says Edie. 'From the shop.'

It won't be the same though. I had such marbellous plans for the gorilla I was going to buy. I was going to call it Etienne after Gigi's boyfriend because he does look like a handsome ape.

'Never mind, Delilah,' says Lucian. 'When you feel what's in my pocket you'll forget all about your gorilla.'

 143

So I do feel what's in it and so does Edie and we both go, 'Wow! Where did you find that?'

'It was on the floor in the boys' toilet. Don't tell anyone.'

So we don't tell anyone and we especially don't tell Horrid Charlotte because she'll tell on him. She is already in a bad mood because she's found something smelly on her tiger coat.

'It's python poo,' says Ben Silverstein.

'Eeughhh!' she squeals. 'I am never ever wearing it again!' and she throws it on the floor and stamps on it until it's dead.

Mrs Mullet tells her not to be so silly and to ask her mummy to wash it, but she says no, she'll have to have a new one now. Good, because then I will be the only one with a tiger coat, which is what should have happened in the first place.

When we get to the gorillas, they're not even there. They are hiding inside their house so that's a bit disappointing.

'I don't care,' says Horrid Charlotte. 'There are no questions about stupid gorillas in the quiz anyway. I've only come here so I can win the tree house.'

'She'd better not win it if it's a tree house,' growls Edie.

Mind you, if she does, she might fall out, so that would be good.

'Get your money ready,' says Mrs Mullet. 'We're going to the gift shop now.'

The gift shop is a marbellous place. There are china giraffes and glass elephants and all sorts of things for

Darren Paisley to break. Mrs Mullet is holding his hand so he can't run about. He doesn't like it one bit, but at least she's let him buy the hairy bird-eating spider.

It isn't real. It has to be wound up with a key, but when Darren lets it go across the floor and it runs over Horrid Charlotte's silly shoe, it looks ever so real. She screams and screams and, even though she's Teacher's Pet, I think Mrs Mullet is getting fed up with her for being such a fusspot.

I buy a pair of socks with a gorilla on and Edie buys a thing that you blow down, which sounds like a owl, and Lucian is just standing by the furry toys when Horrid Charlotte comes marching up and says, 'Um! Lucian Lovejoy, I saw you steal a toy mouse. I'm telling of you.'

And she does and Mrs Mullet says, 'Lucian, have you put a toy mouse in your pocket?'

And he says, 'No. I have not put a toy mouse. I may be a liar, but I am not a feef.'

He shows Mrs Mullet his pockets and she can see that he hasn't got a toy mouse and she gets a bit cross with Charlotte Griggs and says to please stop telling tales.

'But I saw him!' scowls Charlotte.

Only what she saw wasn't a toy mouse. It was a real one, and it didn't live in Lucian's pocket any more, it lived up his jumper. It stayed there ever so happy all the way home on the coach and when it peeped out of his neck hole we fed it bits of Saloni's samosa.

We were so busy with Lucian's dear mouse, we forgot to sing the gorilla song, but I'm so glad Mrs Woolly Hat taught it to me because guess what happened?

When we all got back into our classroom at Wheatfields Infants School, we gave our quiz answers to Mrs Mullet so she could mark them, and when she finished, she said, 'It's a tie!'

Me and Edie were very disappointed because we thought that was the prize and we don't like wearing ties, but Ben Silverstein said, 'Actually, Delilah, a tie means two of us have won. Me and Charlotte most probably.'

'The children who got the same questions right are Charlotte . . . and Delilah!' says Mrs Mullet. 'And as there's only one prize, we will have to have a tiebreaker question.'

In case you don't know, a tiebreaker is when Mrs Mullet gives Horrid Charlotte and me a very hard question and whoever puts their hand up and says the answer first wins.

'Listen carefully,' says Mrs Mullet. 'Here comes the question. Gorillas have special thumbs so they can grasp tools. What word do we use to describe those special thumbs?'

I know the answer! I remember the words to Mrs Woolly Hat's song about gorillas scratching themselves underneath with sticks and I put my hand up and I sing, '*Gorillas' hands are like a man's, they both have* . . . opposable *thumbs!*'

'That's the right answer, Delilah!' says Mrs Mullet. 'Very well done!'

'Oh . . . I knew that,' sulks Charlotte. 'About gorillas having impossible thumbs.'

But she didn't and even if she did I said it first and I have won! The prize isn't a baby elephant or a yacht or even a tree house, but I don't mind. I've got all those things in my Far Away Land so I don't need more of them really.

What I've actually won is the most

marbellous shiny lunch box with the
best ever gorilla on the lid, which is just
what I've always wanted.

'And even Horrid Charlotte hasn't got
one of those,' says Edie.

Where I come from, that has to be the
best prize in the whole universe.

It all started with a Scarecrow

Puffin is well over sixty years old.
Sounds ancient, doesn't it? But Puffin has never been
so lively. We're always on the lookout for the next big
idea, which is how it began all those years ago.

Penguin Books was a big idea from the mind of
a man called Allen Lane, who in 1935 invented
the quality paperback and changed the world.
**And from great Penguins, great Puffins grew,
changing the face of children's books forever.**

The first four Puffin Picture Books were hatched in 1940 and the
first Puffin story book featured a man with broomstick arms called
Worzel Gummidge. In 1967 Kaye Webb, Puffin Editor, started the
Puffin Club, promising to **'make children into readers'**.
She kept that promise and over 200,000 children became
devoted Puffineers through their quarterly installments of
Puffin Post, which is now back for a new generation.

Many years from now, we hope you'll look back and
remember Puffin with a smile. **No matter what your age
or what you're into, there's a Puffin for everyone.**
The possibilities are endless, but one thing is for sure:
whether it's a picture book or a paperback, a sticker book
or a hardback, **if it's got that little Puffin
on it – it's bound to be good.**